THE GUARDIAN

A.L. HAWKE

PHANTOM HEART, LLC

ISBN: 978-1-953919-21-2 (ebook)

ISBN: 978-1-953919-22-9 (paperback)

ISBN: 978-1-953919-23-6 (hardcover)

Library of Congress Control Number: 2022921336

This is a work of fiction. It all comes directly from the imagination of the author's mind. This includes names, characters, places, and incidents. Any public names are used solely for creative purposes. Any resemblance to actual people, living or dead, or to companies, institutions or locales is entirely coincidental or accidental.

Line edited by Stephanie Marshall Ward

Proofread by Alexa B., alexabooks.wixsite.com/authors

Cover © 2022 by Brosedesignz

Published by Phantom Heart, LLC

27702 Crown Valley Pkwy D-4, #201

Ladera Ranch, CA 92694, USA

Printed and bound in the United States of America

First printing December, 2022

Learn more about A.L. Hawke at www.alhawke.com

Correspondence: contact@alhawke.com

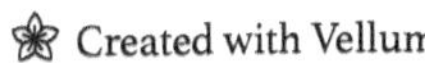 Created with Vellum

Dedicated to my son Evan D.
Arachne was his idea

1

MY MARKER

It's dark, but the water's warm. A green glow shines in front of me. That's the glow from my eyes. The thick black cobras in my hair are stirring on my head like crazy. They don't like water and they know where this is heading. My incisors have grown into fangs, my fingernails are sharp as knives, and my face is wrinkled like an old lady's. Yeah, I'm in full-on Medusa mode. But I probably look pretty silly to the fish as a sea monster swimming in a bathing suit.

Oh, there's a shark. He's a big one. Watch out, sharkie, I've got teeth too. I adore these creatures, by the way. They're cannibals. As a monster myself, I play nice and find eating my own kind to be really gross, but I respect killing machines.

I lost the little fella. I smell him more than see him now. He's giving me a wide breadth. It must be these snakes snapping back at him over my head.

I've changed into Medusa because, honestly, I'm totally freaked out. It's creepy swimming alone in the ocean at night. I'm waiting for a great white shark to latch onto my legs and tug me down, like in that famous scene in *Jaws*. Remember that movie? You know when the girl at the beginning of the movie is, like, laughing while frolicking on the beach, running from her boyfriend, and she goes out on the water alone? She jerks in surprise because a two-ton shark is chomping off her legs. Then she's pulled down, spurting unintelligible things as her whole body is torn apart. I love that scene. Anyway, sharkies, you best not pull that shit on me.

Where's my marker?

The important thing at the moment is finding the statue. It's not much further out, if I remember.

I peek out of the water for a second to catch my breath. I squint as light shines from a tower under the shadow of a hill by the shore. I see a small boat sailing near me.

Duck down!

I duck. Then I snort sea water and the water trickles over my eyes. My boyfriend's snorkeling mask is too large. He's going to hike over to San Fruttuoso Bay and snorkel tomorrow, and he'll be using aquatic equipment during the day like a normal person.

Which will already be wet. Which you'll have to explain to him, Gorgi.

Yeah, whatever, Medusa.

I reposition my leaky mask over my face and look down toward the sea floor. A few scattered fish glow green in the light from my eyes. Other than that, it's just a dark, sandy floor about five meters down. No statue. I gargle more salt water.

Jesus.

Yes, Jesus. Where are you?

I'd really like to return to my dry, warm hotel right now.

I think the effigy is closer to the shore.

One fin at a time, Medusa. One fin at a time.

And there it is! *Christo degli Abissi.*

The Jesus Christ statue is standing on stone steps underwater, with outstretched arms—glowing green from my gaze—looking right up at me. A few small fish are swimming around a small reef behind him. The marker points to the spot. But I need more air to search. Ready? Well...here goes. Now don't laugh, but I can only hold my breath for, like, twenty seconds. That makes me a poor free diver. I catch a quick breath at the surface again, then I dive. As I kick, my body darts like a dolphin toward the statue. My hands brush over the stone hand. Then, using my green gaze, I skim the sandy bottom looking for her entrance.

Do you remember where it is? I can't recall. I mean, the statue's pretty darn popular so it must be hidden. I remember it being near a rocky structure.

Just go back to the hotel.

I have to find her.

After seeing nothing but sand, I force my way back in the other direction. There are no fish around me now because, for a moment, I was choking on sea water and struggling to breathe. I look up. The monument's above me now. Illuminated by my emerald eyes, looking more jade in the dark sea, the statue stands over me in full majesty. He's awe inspiring, and in sunlight, he'd be even better.

I can't breathe!

I rise fast, gulping more water, until I reach the surface again. Again, there's the tower to my side; in the other direction, the sea. I'm far out now. The waves undulate, pushing me up and down, making me feel really queasy. Well, here we go again.

Just go back to the hotel. This is horrible.

I have to find her.

Hey, look! I think it's by those rocks over there beyond the statue.

But I realize my super cursed eyes saw the rock formation, making it appear closer than it really is. Even swimming quickly, it is taking a long time to get there. Far worse, the surface is way up above me now.

I fight myself, air or not, to keep skimming the bottom. I shine my green eyes along the rocks.

Then my body jerks. A huge bolus of fluid comes from my mouth in a bubble and makes me cough, swallowing more and gagging. I squeeze my hands tight to try to remain calm. Then I look at the ocean surface far above me.

Go back up!

I smell humans. I also feel the water stir as they swim overhead. At this time? Can you believe it? They're scuba divers, judging from the bubbles moving around them, about a half mile to my left, where I saw the boat. Well, these divers have a lot of excitement in store, and not just the thrill of seeing the Christo degli Abissi at night, if I'm still here.

Where are you, Arachne!

Hi. Blacked out for a moment. Shit, where's my mask. *Shit!* My lover's going to totally kill me.

~

I'm bobbing up and down in the waves along the surface, coughing up a storm, gasping for air mixed in the salty brine. Was I out again?

~

I'm fucking convulsing.

I catch a glimpse of the statue with my roaming green gaze.

Give up, Gorgiana!

Something tugs at my leg. Something grabs me and I'm yanked down, pulled so hard that my shoulder slams against the sea floor. It reminds me of that scene from *Jaws* again. I'm dragged along the sand moving so fast, as if a boat snagged me on a fishing line and is dragging me. Surrounded by bubbles, I can't see a thing above me. And this rush of water. It burns my eyes. And...I feel pain in my chest again...and...

2

———

BUONDÌ

I OPEN MY EYES AND GAZE UP AT A MUDDY CEILING. Water drips from above and along the walls. And there's a single flickering yellowish-red light. I turn my head and see it's fire. A figure in a black poncho is hunched over it, cooking something in a metal frying pan. I smell cooked fish. She's pale-skinned and bald. Her hand, holding the pan over the fire, is thin, bony, and black.

There's movement under my back. I turn to my side and it tickles me. I lean over to take a look.

I scream! I was lying on thousands of spiders! *Gross!*

"*Buondì*, Medusa," the figure in black says with a chuckle.

Icky spiders scatter about me.

"I hate spiders!"

"Why'd you visit then? Hmm?"

I feel so sick I vomit all over the stupid little bugs, coughing up a torrent of clear water, which washes over and floods them. So there! The sea water rushes out of my nostrils too. I can't breathe. I'm gasping.

I close my eyes. Someone is holding me. I turn and see my friend's eyes by the flickering flames. Arachne's eyes are made up of tiny black dots, but she has normal lips and pretty features. And she's smiling.

"Found you," I say.

"*Benvenuto.* Why'd you come, Medusa?"

"Trouble." Then I barf up more water by her side.

"It will pass," Arachne says, patting my back.

I take a deep breath, inhaling more salt. But then I find that I can breathe. Yeah, *I can breathe!* It's, like, heaven. I stand up straight, taking in more wondrous air. Arachne returns to her fire, lifting a metal frying pan.

"I'm making you breakfast," she says. "Barracuda."

"Oh, yummy."

She shrugs. "It's fresh."

Somehow, the spiders are gone. She commands the little ones, you know. I suppose she was trying to make me comfortable, using them as a mattress, but how disgusting.

I look around her cave. It's only the size of a small room, but it adjoins a muddy hallway. The opposite side of her cave has an antique wood dresser she must have dragged here. And lying about it is a pile of dresses. My friend loves clothes. In the nineteenth century, Arachne was a designer. And before that, she often specialized in fashion. That's how she got cursed in the first place. But the weirdest thing in this muddy lair is not the large, elegant dresser and pile of clothes, it's a pile of filthy, rotting fish lying on the floor full of, not spiders, but—

eek!—worms. You know I love snakes, but when worms are the size of my fingernail—*gross.* This must be, like, her refrigerator or something. She looks back at me, her eyes clusters of small black balls in her normal, pretty face, and smiles again. Her face is lovely—sans the spider eyes.

"You went the wrong way," Arachne says. "The passage was in the opposite direction."

"Figures."

"I told you to never return. You're breaking my vow of silence."

"I had to."

"Why? What is it? What made you drown yourself?"

I take a deep breath. Oh, what a relief it is to breathe again! It's so weird how things like breathing can be taken for granted. My friend can breathe underwater for hours because she is cursed to be in the form of a spider, and spiders can stay underwater for a long time. Not snakes. Only a few snakes can swim and hold their breath. And certainly not good ole Medusa. You know, I can only hold my breath for twenty seconds.

"The war's back. Imada is coming for you."

Arachne moves the sizzling meat in her pan and shakes her head. "The war will never end."

"Hades got information from Athena." When I utter the goddess's name, Arachne's arm holding the pan shakes. "Athena blabbed that you know the location of the Scepter. Then she told him you were here. That information leaked and now you have Imada after you. You know the Scepter of Azure's power. Imada wants the staff. As far as we know, it's the only Scepter left."

"Now I understand all those divers swimming

around the cave lately. I thought you were one of them with a green flashlight."

"You picked a popular spot. No one's found this place yet?"

"And no one will." She shakes her head, still crouched staring at her frying pan. "This cave is not near the statue. No one will find the entrance, unless I will it."

"Where's the Scepter of Azure, Arachne?"

"Breakfast is ready. I caught a small one. It should be very good. Buon appetito."

She walks over and hands me the pan with a smile. I take it to be polite.

"I'm so happy you came," Arachne says, touching my arm.

Her multi-dot eyes can turn green like mine, you know. But while normal, mine are beautiful, hers are ugly. But both are just as repulsive, just for different reasons. She doesn't look straight into my eyes because she knows my curse—I freeze whoever stares at them. I look down. But then I look over at her slaughterhouse wall stash.

And she's still waiting for me to eat.

"Barracuda?" I ask.

Arachne nods.

"I really wouldn't want to impose."

"There's plenty. Go ahead."

I can't stop smelling the wall of rotten fish. Then I look at the slimy cooked fish, gills and all, in the pan. Yum. To be polite, I sit on her damp, muddy floor beside her. I tear off a piece of white flesh and eat around the scales. She's still all smiley watching me. *Here goes...*

"It's good," I say with my mouth full. It really isn't bad.

"Yeah," she says. tearing some from the pan. "Everything is better down here."

"It's been so long," I say, touching her arm. "I miss you."

She nods. Then she puts an arm around me. "I miss you more, Medusa. Of all people, I miss you the most."

"Are you really happy here?"

"It's home." She shrugs. Then she looks around her room. "I'm far happier here than I could ever be up there. Up there is Athenia."

"Cora defeated her," I say, shaking my head. "Mount Olympus was—"

She shakes her head, losing her smile. Then the little balls in her eyes shine emerald, like my eyes did underwater.

"Let's not start up with that again," she snaps. "The Hellenistic world you reside in was created by her."

"But Hades and Cora run the show now."

"No."

She jumps up.

"No."

Her eyes have turned even brighter green. Her legs and arms narrow a little and she's a little taller. She's lengthening, changing into a spider. She does this, just like my hair turns into thick snakes when I get worked up.

"Apollo and Athena hold sway over your world," she says, avoiding my eyes. "Even if you don't see it, they and their slaves run Gaia. You're deluding yourself, just like your best friend Persephone, Cora, is deluded."

"I didn't come to fight. I came to get you out of here."

"I will never leave. I have my family of darlings. And I have my idol. I'm happy and in peace. I suspect I'm happier than you. You came for Cora's Scepter? Even if I had it, I wouldn't give it to you. I love you, Medusa, I really do, but you know I'm Christian. I believe in End Times. I'll go on praying in my sanctuary under my god, but I will never risk being the instrument of his apocalypse."

"Cora knew you wouldn't give it to her. But if you give it to me, Imada will have no more reason to search for you."

"I don't have it."

I squint at her. I don't believe her. Her black smock is shining green, this time in the glow of my eyes.

"If you give me the staff, I'll get rid of it," I add. "I'll hide it so no one can find it. Cora promised. She knows her prophecy. She doesn't want the prophecy to come true either."

"Then it will be found," she says, shaking her head. "I'm not only worried about Persephone, I'm worried that it will be found by someone else and used to hurt people."

"You have to trust me."

She sits by the fire again, with her back turned to me, and tears more fish from the pan and just eats. "No." But she smiles again. "Have breakfast with me and let us speak of other pleasant things. Please, Medusa."

"I didn't come here for the Scepter. I came for you."

"I'm fine. But even if they find me..." she says, chewing with her mouth full. "They will never get the Scepter."

"So you do have it?"

Arachne sighs deeply. I sit down beside her and rub her back. "Oh, Arachne, aren't you miserable here? Let me take you back to the surface."

"Don't pity me!" she exclaims, shaking her head hard. "Don't ever do that! That's acting like them. Do you think that if I had crossed your friend Persephone, she wouldn't have cursed me too!"

"Cora hates her family more than anyone. She's good. And she can help you."

"Oh, stop, Medusa!" She glares at me with green eyes. But I know my eyes are green too, because her face shines green. "How is Cora good? She killed everyone she loved." She points a finger at her other skeletal hand. Her arms are dried up, like a corpse's. "You can't go outside under the sun, but look at me? Look at my hands. Or my eyes." She points to all those black dots making up her spider eyes. Then she slaps her hand along her bald head. "You have snakes for hair? So? At least you have hair. They did this to us. They *all* did this to you and me. They're not our friends, they're responsible. I don't trust any of them. All of them, including your Kore, are overbearing, pompous, sadistic. You had beauty, I had skill. So? They made us monsters. But they kept you human enough to delude you. Now you come here because that bitch holds you as if by a leash."

I growl at her. That makes me so mad, and she knows it. She backs up as my lion roar echoes in her cave. Now she's against the wall. She's grown taller in spider form, but she's lanky and rigid and she knows, in a fight, I could crush her like a bug.

"I'm ruined, Medusa!" Arachne says, holding up a hand. "Ruined. There's no hope for me. Maybe you've made your peace with gods, but my plight is hopeless. I have only one God. And I'm happy praying to him in peace. Just go and leave me alone."

"But you're in danger here, Arachne! You have to leave for your safety!" I turn my back to her and fold my arms, because I'm ready to pulverize her. My snakes are moving wildly, snapping at her from behind my head. I have to calm down but—

A LEASH! A LEASH! She always fucking provokes you. What difference does it make who's more miserable? Why don't you shatter her peace with her God, Gorgi, and fucking squash her like the bug she is.

Arachne touches my back. "I'm sorry, Medusa. I'm sorry. But they're all bad. This talk always leads to unpleasantness with us. Let us just have barracuda and speak of pleasant things. Please."

"You have to let me take you back to the surface," I say, shaking my head. "I offer you protection. You're not safe here. Hades and Cora told me Imada are coming. I agreed to come only for you, not the stupid Scepter. I came to take you somewhere safe."

"I'm not leaving."

I cock my head back. She's not lanky anymore. She's turning human. And her eyes are back to being black, not green.

"I won't speak of this again," Arachne says. "Have breakfast and come tell me about America. I want to know how you've been all these years. I've missed you."

"There's not much to say." I force a smile. "I'm

living in a college town named Sunland in Florida in the States. I'm working in a library."

"*Bene.* Away from people. I understand."

"No. I work there so I can observe people while I work late at night."

She furrows her brow and considers that for a moment, nodding silently. She'd never understand that. She's always been an obstinate recluse, even when she lived up on the surface.

"I also met someone," I add.

"*Fantastico,*" Arachne says with a laugh. "Is he cute, Medusa?"

"Yes. And I love him."

"Does he know what you are?"

"Yes."

"Ah, much better."

"Any man in your life, Arachne?"

"No. But I have God." Did you figure out yet that Arachne is a zealot? Why do you think she has a large underwater statue of Jesus in her front yard? "I am so happy to see you, Medusa." She smiles at me, running her hand down my arm. "Of all people in this world, you have the most pure heart. I am so happy you've come. I don't want to fight."

"I don't either."

"*Bene.*" She takes me into her arms and hugs me tight. Then she gazes at my hair and runs her hand through it. "What about you? Are *you* happy?"

"Yes."

"*Tutto bene.* I live my simple life. You have your man in sun city. And I have my little darlings."

She gestures toward a wall. I didn't notice before, but a whole pile of spiders is scurrying near a crack and crawling up the wall. Some are large, but most are tiny, and there are so many of them that they've shadowed a section of the room. Yet they're all in one spot, controlled by her. When I look back at my friend, I try very hard not to look totally grossed out.

"*Benvenuto in Italia*, Medusa," she says with a chuckle.

"Thank you. But—" I look at the icky spider. "Honestly, I think it's better up at the surface, Arachne."

"It isn't."

3

———

BREAKFAST

I tried to bring a special breakfast to my lover for in-room dining. I didn't want to wake him. Honestly, I'm exhausted. I was up all night. That's okay because that's my normal wakey time, but I think I'm still a little traumatized by drowning.

When I slip into a nightgown, yawn, crawl into bed, and gaze out over our open balcony, facing a glorious view of the sun over the sea, my lover puts his arm around me. And that feels nice. As he spoons me, his hand wanders over my shoulder and inside my soft silk nightgown. That feels nicer. I turn for easy access. I even scoot a little closer, with my butt touching his body.

"I thought you were sleeping," I say, as his fingers sneak under my bra and along the curve of my breast.

"Where were you, Gorgi?"

I push his hand back, scoot up on our soft bed, and pull off my nightgown. Then, just wearing a bra and panties, I lie back in bed. But I don't put my head down on the pillow until I take in another gorgeous view of the Italian Riviera shining through the doors to our balcony. It's so beautiful. To the side, rectangular buildings with three or four stories of windows reflect the rays of the brightening red dawn. *Bello*, as the locals say. Yellow lights come from those buildings and from docked ships shining along the water. And there's a red glow on the horizon. I think of my spider friend and the irony that she chose to live in such an amazing place but prefers gazing at the statue of her god underwater to the most beautiful scenery in the world.

"I got you breakfast, babe," I say. "Juice, cappuccino, and biscotti. It's totally Italy."

"I can't wait," he says, kissing my neck.

He keeps kissing me. I don't think he wants an Italian breakfast, to tell you the truth. I think he wants Ancient Greek. Me.

He tugs at my panties. Yeah. I help him by pulling them off and throwing them off the bed.

"Where were you?" he asks, kissing my neck again.

"With another man."

He stops kissing me.

"Just a joke," I say with a laugh.

"That's not funny." But he laughs. "Really, Gorge, we were so tired, I was surprised to see you not at the hotel."

"I couldn't sleep and I didn't want to disturb you."

I'm cursed, you know. I can't show my hair outside because the sun shows my snakes moving under my hair. But they don't come out at night. So I often walk along the beach back home while my boyfriend sleeps. So my excuse isn't that hard for him to believe.

"I heard you shower."

"Yeah, I wanted to smell good for you. Kiss me."

And I lean back and pucker up. He quickly closes his eyes to avoid my gaze. It's dark in the room but glowing a bit green from my desire. Maybe it's dark enough to not curse him with my poisonous gaze, but I've trained him not to chance it.

I feel his body press closer against me.

"You're not going to tell me where you went?" he asks, running his lips along my arm. Shit, I want to. But I feel like the less he knows, the less trouble he'll get into. "You don't have to," he says. Then I feel his lips and stubble wander over my neck, and I laugh because it tickles. He fingers my bra. "This place is amazing." He turns to our balcony. So do some of my wigglies in my hair. It's okay if he feels the movement. He knows by now about my fucking cursed snakes and monster identity.

"You still think I shouldn't have come with you?"

Yes.

He unclasps my bra just in time to ask me that. That makes me chuckle again. As I hear him removing his underwear, the answer's pretty obvious, isn't it. Especially when he slowly enters me with his cock. But, yeah, he shouldn't have come.

Fuck, that feels good...

He tricked me. I told him I had to go to Europe for a friend, and he snatched my ticket from me and studied it. Before I knew it, I found him running down the loading bridge at the airport with luggage over his shoulder. Then he was sitting next to me. Yeah, he even bought a seat next to mine. He thought he was just being fun. He didn't know the kind of friend I was visiting or how much trouble she was in. So there I was, stuck with a choice between demanding that he get off the plane and letting him come with me. So...

Fuck...that feels soooo good. Well, what is a girl to do? Right?

"Oh, God," I say with a moan. "Yes. I'm very happy you're here."

He laughs. "You're so funny."

"Why are you always saying I'm funny?"

"Because you're making love to me while cracking jokes."

"Actually, you kinda started that one."

He's groping my breasts, squeezing, while pushing into me. He squeezes a bit too hard, but that's okay—it tells me I'm driving him wild. I am arguably the most beautiful girl that ever was, you know—sans the snakes and fangs. His fingers play with my erect nipples. Then I feel my stupid hair moving even more.

He groans.

"I have some bad news," I say, as he repositions. He moves his weight right on top of me, but he turns his head to avoid my petrifying gaze. Then I run my hands along the hard muscles of his back and arms. He runs his lips along my cheek with more kisses. A snake or two drifts by, but he doesn't seem to notice or care.

"What?" he breathes. "What is it?"

"I lost your snorkeling mask."

"What!" he snaps. He actually stops moving. "You did? How?" He almost stares into my green eyes, he gets so worked up.

"I left it in a bag when we got off the train," I lie. Geesh, I didn't know he'd care *that* much.

"That was prescription, babe. I don't think they'll have that here."

"I'm sorry. We can check with the concierge."

"They won't have it," he says, shaking his head.

"Your vision isn't that bad." And I run my palm across the stubble of his cheek. He turns from my gaze, and I light his face green with my desire.

"But I really wanted to see the Christo degli Abissi."

He closes his eyes. I chuckle again because he sounds like a tantruming kid. I cradle his head.

"I told you, I saw the one in Florida. This is the original. I wanted to see it with clear eyes." *It wasn't all that great in the dark.* "Yesterday you were telling me you could skip snorkeling altogether since we couldn't go together," I object. "Now you're mad?"

"I know. But...you got me all excited over seeing it."

"We'll figure out something. Maybe we can fit you with glasses inside a mask or something."

"You can't do that." His hand runs along my hip, and he's still lying on me. He kisses my cheek. Then he does what I rarely let any man do—he runs his fingers through my hair. "Oh...forget it. You're right. I'm being stupid." He caresses the curves of my breasts. I rise and kiss his lips. Then I dance my tongue with his. He stops kissing me for a moment and looks behind him, gazing at the rays of yellow from the rising sun. "This is the most amazing place I've ever seen."

"And you're the most amazing man I've ever been with." I pull his hard body closer to me. "Now get back to doing what you were doing, mister."

"We could snorkel together at night," he says. "It's warm enough."

"Are you crazy! Who snorkels in the middle of the night?"

Giggles.

4

SWANK

I'M SITTING IN THIS CUTE FORMAL BLACK DRESS AT A table right beside the dock. My hair's all natural, hanging down to my shoulders. I combed the little wigglies down and they're neatly tucked underneath my curls. My face is dolled up and pretty for my lover. But I'm wearing really thick ugly glasses so nobody gets hypnotized by a stray glance.

Portofino è bellisimo.

I mean, right? The sky is clear, the stars are peeking through a purple-yellow glow lighting the horizon, and the classic yellow, pink, and red buildings by the Mediterranean Sea are turning nighttime yellow. All those yachts and fishing boats are brightening up too.

I sip white wine. Then I sigh. It would all make a wonderful vacation if I weren't so worried about my friend.

"Not here yet?"

I tear my eyes from the gorgeous view. It's my waiter, this clean-cut young guy in a suit and tie. I shake my head, quickly avoiding his gaze by looking down at the tablecloth.

"Would you like to order an appetizer, senora? Spiedino or caprese? Or perhaps oysters? *È Buonissimo.*"

He has an English accent. I don't think he's local, more like working for the tourist trade. You know this is a tourist town. Of course, I'm fluent in Italian.

"Prendo una focaccia al formaggio, per favore."

"*Magnifico,*" he says, bringing his fingers to his lips.

This guy's cute. He's young and well built and the smile under his mustache reveals nice teeth. He leaves me looking at the harbor again. Many pretty boats are docked, and the purple-orange horizon is fading to black.

I've been here for half an hour. I really don't care, just as long as my lover's all right and I have this view. He went snorkeling like a normal human this afternoon.

A guy at another table looks over at me. His button-down gapes open, revealing part of his chest, and his sleeves are rolled up to his elbows. His blond date is sitting by him sipping champagne. She's got a chignon and an elegant black dress. The guy is gazing right at me. I quickly look down. This is all I need—to make a scene freezing some stranger in the restaurant.

That happened to me in Paris once. It was a busy café, and two guys, sitting with their friends, were staring at me. Their mouths were gaping open for like thirty seconds, and people thought they were having a stroke or something. It was such a scene, with sirens blaring from an ambulance. Anyway, look away from Medusa. Look away.

I mean it. Don't look at me!

An older couple sits at another table on the dock, not dressed too fancy, just enjoying the view like me. This couple looks cute together, but a bit too casually dressed. I love that.

I sip more of this delicious sweet white wine. In my periphery, the guy's still looking over. Worse, he has a ring on his left hand. So does his wife, who's now ignoring him, staring at the door to the inside of the restaurant.

I run a finger along the top of my wine glass. Then I sigh again. It's such a lovely view. I regret not bringing one of my cheap, silly romance paperbacks from home to read while waiting for my man.

Finally, the table shakes as the seat across from me is taken. He's here!

No... wait... This doesn't smell like my boyfriend.

"Medusa," a young girl across from me says. "It's been too long."

But she's not a young girl. She's that bitch goddess.

"No, it really hasn't," I reply. "It hasn't been long enough."

Unlike all the humans around us, I glare right into her bright blue eyes, now glistening in the candlelight. But I shake a little. This goddess hates me as much as I hate her. Her hair's long and black, her olive skin is similar to mine, but that's, thankfully, where our similarities end. Her hair is curled too much, like a perm. She's wearing stinky perfume. She's got her face caked in too much makeup. She's trying to look older. She always has. She's been trying to look older her whole damned eternal life. She always wants to look like her favorite sister, Athena, who she practically worships. The thing is, she's always seemed like a cheap, immature copy of Athene. And, although both goddesses look young, this goddess's features seem locked in teenagedom.

The little bitch's infernal name is Diana. Once she was known as Artemis. She is the goddess of the moon, a very unfair appellation for such an ugly creature.

"What brings you to Europe, my pet?" Diana asks, glancing at the dock.

"I'm not your pet!"

She says that just to piss me off. And it does. All the gods know that I'm sensitive about being called an animal. Just like Arachne knew saying "led by a leash" would trigger me.

Diana twirls her fingers and her stupid gold bracelets clang.

"Last I heard, you were in America, Medusa. Florida, I discovered. I spoke to your champion recently. Athena sends her regards."

"There's no way you spoke to her."

Diana leans forward and her eyes flicker red. "Oh, you'd be surprised what I'm capable of."

"What do you want with me?" But I'm really not worried about me. I'm worried about my boyfriend.

"If you give me what I want," Diana says with a shrug, "I won't lay a hand on him." *Who said anything about "HIM"!* "I really don't care about you, Medusa. Just tell me why your master, Kore, sent you here."

"No one sent me. I'm on vacation." I point to the bay. "See?" Then I raise my glass of wine. "Holiday."

She smirks. Then she wags a finger. Her stupid wrist full of gold bracelets rattles again. "She's using you."

Didn't you notice, Gorgi, what she said? She said, "I won't lay a hand on "HIM"!

"Senora, I see you have company." The waiter's standing over Diana. Diana looks up surprised. Apparently, she was too busy hating me to notice him come over. "Would you like a drink?" He smiles at her profile. Of course, Diana is stunningly beautiful. We immortals are all cursed with loveliness.

"Of course," Diana says to the waiter. "I'll have a Sidecar with cognac—cognac from the last century."

"Sí, signora," he says with wide open eyes. "I'll check to see if we can accommodate. If not the last century, it will be of the highest quality, I promise. *Dilizioso.*"

"I should hope so," Diana says. "This is the best restaurant in the Italian Riviera, is it not?"

"We shall satisfy your desires." Then he does that cute kiss gesture with his fingers and darts off, happy to get her hoity-toity cocktail order. The goddess chuckles with conceit, checking him out as he walks back inside the restaurant.

"Pretentious bitch," I say under my breath.

"Why were you sent here?" Diana snaps, turning back to me. She's got Cora's bright blue eyes. They're pretty on Cora, but hideous on her. I swallow my delicious wine. It's such a dichotomy to be in a beautiful restaurant with such a pompous young cunt.

"I wanted to say hi to my friend," I reply. "I told her you guys are coming after her."

Diana responds by shaking her head with more fake grinning. "What friend?"

"As if you didn't know."

"Where is she hiding The Scepter of Azure, Medusa?"

"Diana!" cries a woman's voice. "I don't believe it. You're here too? What a small world."

I jump from my seat. I'm so scared of Diana that my predator sense wasn't paying attention to my surroundings. A gorgeous woman in a long, flowing red dress, long blond hair, and large gold earrings, carrying a small diamond purse, glides over. She sits in a chair beside me and winks. It's Cora, the goddess Persephone, my best friend!

Diana scoots her seat closer to the water, away from Cora. Actually, it looks like she's ready to jump over the rail into the bay.

"What a treat that you're in town," Cora lies to the bitch. "Hi Gorgi." Cora nods at me with a genuine smile. "Sorry I'm late. What a lovely night. The sky is clear and this bitch's moon is nearly full."

The waiter comes over and hands Diana her ridiculously expensive cocktail. "Last century," he says with a wink. Diana doesn't look like she believes him. "Focaccia al formaggio," he says, handing me my appetizer.

"Would you like a drink, signora?" he asks Cora.

"I sure would. A vodka martini."

He smiles and nods. Then he leaves us.

Cora leans over and glares at Diana. "So, what did I miss? What have you two been talking about?"

Diana turns uncomfortably to the dock. Meanwhile Cora glares at her. Diana's silhouette turns a shade red, reflecting the light from my friend's eyes.

"Why are you here?" Diana asks, sipping her snooty drink, with her back still turned to Cora.

"I'm watching over my friend," Cora replies. "The important question is, what are *you* doing here? Last I heard you were caring for a private island off the coast of Spain. The owner just disappeared, didn't she?"

"Is this really the place for a fight?" Diana snaps quietly.

"Who's fighting?" Cora says with a laugh. "I'm hungry." She reaches over and grabs some of my bread. I don't eat any. I'm losing my appetite.

"The spider is my business, not yours," Diana says, finally facing Cora. I shudder at her bright red eyes. "I get that you protect this snake. But the spider's fate should not be your concern. She has no allegiance to anyone."

"Arachne was changed by Athena too!" I snap.

"We saw you in the water last night, Medusa," Diana says, turning to me. "She's obviously down there. You didn't swim alone in the middle of the night to see the monument. It'd save us a lot of time if you told me her exact location. Then I can just go."

"I don't even know," I say. And that's the truth. I was led on a route that's far from the statue and then down a hallway to an exit with an impassible current. And there's no way I'll ever enter the way I exited.

"Did she have the scepter?" Diana asks.

"She didn't tell me," I say to both of them. "She said that even if she did, she'd never tell anyone."

"Unlike you, Kore," Diana blurts out, "even spiders aren't interested in destroying the world." Diana sits back in her chair and sips her snooty drink again. "If you want to know why I'm here, it's to stop you from getting your hands on that weapon."

"Liar," Cora says. "I have no interest in it. Your friends do."

"Anything that destroys our peace is in your interest," Diana objects. "It's in your nature as queen of the Underworld. It's just a matter of time before your disease from beneath the ground is unearthed again."

"How poetic, but untrue," Cora objects. "You and your fucked organization won't relent in screwing the world."

"I'm not a part of Imada."

"There's another lie," Cora says.

The waiter returns and hands Cora her martini.

Cora sips it and waits for the waiter to leave. Then she says, "I'm not planning to destroy the world, Diana. But I'm not going to let you hurt my friend."

"Your destruction of my home proves you will, sister!" Diana says, hitting the table. "Your prophecy from your own lips says you will!"

All the couples and families at nearby tables turn. And their stares finally make Cora and Diana cover their red eyes. I catch a glimpse of that man who was ogling me. He's furrowing his brow, and he and his wife are staring curiously.

"Shut up," Cora snaps quietly. She and Diana shield their red eyes from everyone's stares. "Stop making a scene. I thought only Athena was stupid enough to try to expose us."

"You rile me up, sister," Diana says with a shrug. But she's talking more quietly. "You always did. You and your beastly husband have brought our family to ruin." Then Diana turns to me. The red is shining through cracks between her fingers. "If you tell us where the scepter is, I'll leave. I'll even let the spider go."

"Arachne won't tell me," I say. "She holds the same fears you do about Cora. Isn't it enough to know that nobody knows where it is? If Arachne has it, she won't ever use it."

"Tell me," Diana says, releasing her fingers from her face and staring at me. "If you don't, I'm game for a fight."

"Oh, you could never take me on, Artemis," Cora says with a laugh. "And you're not getting anywhere with Medusa *and* me here together."

But then Diana smiles. She gestures toward the beach. A large group of black suits with shades are standing there. Two guys are talking into walkie-talkies on their shoulders. Their long black coats could be concealing guns. I'm just glad my boyfriend isn't here.

But he will be! Which is why you have to leave now, Gorgi!

I know, Medusa. I know.

You have to quickly end this!

"I thought you weren't a part of Imada?" Cora asks Diana, gazing curiously over my shoulder at her army. "What's your plan? You want to kill a bunch of bystanders eating dinner? Why are you bringing them here?"

"That's up to you. If Medusa fesses up, nothing will happen at all."

"I told you, I don't know!" I cry. "Okay. She didn't say!"

Now I'm covering my green eyes in rage. I'm looking down and, with all the eyes staring down at our tablecloth, it's looking like some sort of perverse Christmas decoration.

The cloth moves and the table shakes again as the last seat is taken. God, tell me it's not my date!

"Am I late for this meeting, ladies?"

Diana looks up and her eyes look like they're about to burst from their sockets. I recognize that awful voice. I'd recognize it anywhere. It's Hades. He's in a black suit and tie with short dark hair. It's a wig. He's naturally bald like Arachne. And he's got a beard.

The sun's down. There's a lovely moon shining, and the stars are out. It's quiet, because we're all in shock. In the flickering candlelight, the setting is perversely romantic and perfect for my lover, but the strangest setting possible for an Olympic showdown.

My hair's getting jumpy. I take a tie from my purse and quickly tie it in a bun. It's the hardest bun I've ever tied in my life.

"Hello Kore, my lovely," Hades says, sitting near me. "Medusa. Hello. And greetings to our criminal." He wags a finger at Diana. "Diana, I haven't seen you in years. What a wondrous reunion to see you here again tonight. I wonder why."

Diana sends some kind of hand signal to the black-suited men that makes them disperse.

"Would you like a drink, senor?" the waiter asks Hades.

"*Lasciaci, lasciaci,*" Hades snaps, waving his hand dismissively at the waiter. Hades leans over the table. "Cut the shit, shall we, Diana? The scepter's mine. I gave it to the nymphs, sure, but it was made for me. I own it and when it is found, it will be returned to me.

You've always been a little girl looking up to the big boys. Well, I still hold your boss and—"

"Will you just shut up," Cora says, rolling her red eyes. "We've got enough dicks blazing, we didn't need the biggest one in the world to come here."

"Looks like you did, Kore."

"She doesn't have it," Cora says. "Nobody's getting our scepter because Arachne's not even telling Gorgiana."

"Then why the fuck are they here?" Hades asks, pointing to the men in black retreating.

"I thought she had it," Diana says with a shrug. She sips her drink. "I'm still not so sure she doesn't."

"I don't know where the scepter is, okay?" I repeat, exasperated.

Where's my date?!

There's a shriek. It's Diana. She nearly falls off her chair, pointing at the table with wide open eyes. In the center, crawling along the white tablecloth, is a large black tarantula. All the gods look at each other, even the ones who hate one another. Then they all smile. This can only mean one thing: Arachne.

But she can't appear now! Not in front of them. They'll hurt her. It's nearly as bad as my date showing up.

"I didn't come here for your stupid weapon, 'kay?" I cry, jumping up. "I came here because Cora told me my friend Arachne is in trouble. I wanted to help my friend. But you know what, Cora? I'm not even so sure she's not in trouble because of you. Maybe Arachne's right. Maybe there's no side to be on."

They all look up at me. All of them except Hades, who's staring at the creepy spider.

"You hold the world's wealth and power in your hands," I rage on, "but you can't get along for a second. Your family. All you do is bring down all the people around you. It's what you guys have been doing forever. Athene changed Arachne because she couldn't take anyone being better at making clothes. Just as she cursed me for my hair. You don't act like people, you act like animals. You cursed me and then you cursed Arachne."

"I really hate spiders," Diana says, ignoring me and staring back at the creepy thing about to crawl over Cora's salad dish. "Does this mean she's here, Hades? Is she?" Then the bitch jumps and screams again. Another spider creeps up the tablecloth, near her hand. "*I hate spiders!*"

"Show yourself, Arachne," Hades says with a grin, looking around the patio.

"*Why can't you just leave her alone!*" I shout at Hades. This makes Hades finally turn to me. He's got this infernal grin. "Diana, I left Athena alone. Okay? I don't want to be anyone's enemy. All you guys scare me —not for myself, I'm scared about what will happen to my friends! Leave Arachne and me the fuck alone!"

I stop. I'm breathing so heavily. My heart is racing. My whole body's shaking, I'm so pissed. All the gods are silent, staring up at me. But that's good because they're ignoring the creepy-crawly arachnids. But then Cora points at my hair. The wigglies have burst right out of my bun and have turned into thick snakes, going crazy around my head.

A light shines from a cellphone by a nearby table. The phone's being held up high from a guy's outstretched arm, directed at me. I run as fast as the bulb of his cellphone flash, grab it, and smash the phone on the ground under my foot. Everyone in the restaurant gasps. Then I throw my high heels over the rail into the water, so I can run barefoot out of the restaurant while everybody stares. I run alongside the bay, away from Diana's army, until I find a door to an emptier restaurant. Then I endure more gasps as another group of humans see me and my fucking hair.

"Get these creepy things away!" cries stupid Diana back at the first restaurant. I can still hear her with my predator ears. "They're all over the floor!"

I run through an alley and make my way up the hill, moving as fast as I can because my hair is still in full-on snake mode. Did anyone else get a photo? Well, these days, it'll probably be assumed to be fake. That's the funny thing about our secrets. It's rare that humans actually think we're bona fide monsters.

"Where are you going, Kore?" Hades asks. I hear him with my super ears as I rush to my hotel.

"I'm leaving," Cora replies. "I have to apologize to my friend."

"Oh, and you?" asks Hades. "You going somewhere, Diana? I think you and I need to have a word."

"You've got nothing on me, Orcus—unlike everyone else in the family whose lives you've ruined."

"Stay a while. I'm sure I'll find something."

I maneuver around a building and into a dark alley. That's good because everyone, like everyone, is staring at my hair. Finally, I'm far enough away to not hear their stupid infant banter. Their words turn into whispers and then...nothing. The sound of lovely silence.

I reach my hotel room before I know it. I dig in my

pocket for the key card. I insert it and rush into my room.

My man is staring out at the view of the harbor, fixing his tie. He looks so cute in his formal black clothes. He swings around as I run into the room, but he knows to turn from my gaze.

I quickly check my head. Hair is back to normal. The snakes are moving a lot, but they're deep inside.

I run into his arms.

"What's the matter?" he asks. "I was just going to rush down to the restaurant. God, I'm so sorry, Gorge, I'm running late."

I'm not. I couldn't be happier. I kiss his cheek a few times and hug him tight.

"O-k-a-y," he says with a chuckle. "Something wrong?"

"No. I just love you so much." I back up a little and cover his eyes and kiss him on the lips. His face is a little green, but I'm calming down. "Can we just order room service tonight, babe? Is that okay? I decided I'd rather not go out."

"Oh," he says. "Is it because I got back so late?"

"No. I just really want to enjoy the view from our balcony with you alone."

"Sure, I guess. I was excited for that restaurant, but there's nothing more beautiful than this, I suppose."

"Yeah. This view is so pretty. But you don't have to change. We can stay formal. It'll be, like, fun, right? Like a private fancy restaurant. I mean, the restaurant's right on the water. We can eat up here instead and enjoy the amazing view. It can be like breakfast."

"Why do I have the feeling you're hiding something from me?" he asks.

I try to make things light by chuckling. I back up and look at his face. The green glow is gone. He still doesn't look at my eyes because he's too busy looking away. I've trained him well.

He sighs and shrugs. "Sure, Gorge. If that's what you want."

"How was the statue under the water, babe?" I am in his arms.

"It was so cool. It was incredible with the sun shining from above. I even held my breath and dived down near it. I'm really loving this trip. Thank you."

"Even without the prescription mask?"

"Yeah, it was awesome."

"I'm so glad you're enjoying yourself."

That makes one of us, at least.

5

THE WALK

I'M CLIMBING BACK UP THE HILL FROM THE HOTEL, ALONE, to the lighthouse. You know I hiked the same trail a few hours ago with my boyfriend, but he petered out and went to bed. Well, I didn't get to enjoy it long enough. Remember how incredible the view was?

Here's the main square, lit only by a handful of windows and walkway lights. It's almost deserted this early in the morning. There's only a guy putting up a T-shirt display and another man carrying a large box into the patio of an outdoor restaurant. I meander on a path further up the hill. But then I feel a tug from my hair pushing me backward. I stop and turn, looking toward the harbor.

Was that one of you wigglies? Yeah? Get back in there!

I brush the wily snake deeper into my hair. But then I see why I was stopped. The view at this height is amazing. Look at all those buildings, their rectangular windows lit up by the full moon and reflecting over the water. Some of the larger ships and sailboats are lit up yellow. One yacht's floodlight glows aquamarine along the water. I look up and see the clear sky. The stars are twinkly and simply gorgeous.

Sigh.

I should stand here and wait for the sun to rise. But I want to get higher. I like walking at night alone, you know. There's something soothing about just walking and not thinking of much. I mean, aside from a word or two with you. I even love walking along the beach back home in Florida around midnight, when it's warm and clear and beautiful like it is this morning.

Of course, I can't get my mind off Arachne. What was she doing tonight at the restaurant? Why did she leave her house? I'm so worried. I'm about ready to go back to that underwater statue.

You better not.

I sigh again.

"Medusa."

Was that you?

"Medusa," repeats a voice in almost a whisper. I'd recognize that voice anywhere. It's my friend Arachne.

"Where are you?"

I squint in the direction of some olive trees and brush. It sounds as if she's a few steps from me. But... No. Her voice is down below in the direction of the harbor. I think she's miles from me.

"I'm by the bay."

The bay that's a mile down below, she means. I think she's close to the restaurant where Cora's beastly family joined me for dinner and pissed me off last night.

"I'm so sorry you were embarrassed, Medusa. I saw the whole thing."

"I don't care about me. I just didn't want them to harm you. Why'd you do that trick with the spiders?"

There's silence. Then I hear a whimper. Coming from miles away, it's so faint for even my super ears. I tune out a thousand voices at a time back home in busy Sunland, but I can discern voices I recognize when they're talking right at me. I've even freaked out my boyfriend a few times with my magical ability to snoop. Here, in this rural town, it's easy for me to hear Arachne's voice. But I still have to move my wigglies from my ear. It's really weird to hear her few words mixed with complete silence. I almost feel like I'm imagining her voice.

"They destroyed everything," she finally says. "Everything. They set explosives along the sea floor near the cave. There's nothing left of my home."

"Oh, Arachne. I'm so sorry."

I raise my head and sniff for her. I undo my hair clip and risk my snakes being seen in public. It's so early in the morning, but there could still be a few people walking about. But I have to zero in. I see a green schemata of her. She's in human form, wearing a long wig and a black dress. Her arms are hanging over a rail by the bay as she looks at the ships in the harbor. In one hand, she's carrying a knife. Or a cross?

The greatest mystery is how she knew I'd be here. Has she been following me since the restaurant?

"Are you in trouble?" I ask.

"No, they're in trouble."

What does that mean?

"I'm going to get back at them," she says. But then her tone softens. "Portofino reminds me of my home, Colophon, Medusa. Or your home island, Sarpedon, no? It always reminds me of home when I rise to the surface. That's why I live here. Resort towns are not disturbed by modern life. I love this place. That's why I've lived here for so many years."

"Yes, it's beautiful."

"*Sì*. Now I must leave."

Then she falls quiet again. I listen to the crickets. After a very long silence, I repeat, "Why, are *they* in trouble, Arachne?"

"Go back to your vacation with that man of yours. Enjoy yourself. Then return to your city of the sun. This shouldn't involve you. It's between me and them."

"We're at war and I'm on your side, Arachne. I told you that. The fight is very much about me. I came here to protect you. Cora came to protect you too."

"No." She moves from the rail.

"Don't leave."

"I have the Scepter," she says. "I'm going to use it. I planned for an attack at the restaurant before you distracted them. I can wield the Scepter just like Cora once did. She hurt Athena by going after her agents in Spain. I can do the same to Apollo's goons. With the weapon, I could have frozen everyone in the restaurant. The only thing stopping me was my fear of harming the innocent. But the gods need to see my power. And... I have a plan."

"No, Arachne. No. They'll hurt you."

"I don't care."

They'll tear her apart. They can literally tear her limb from limb or watch her burn. It's true, Arachne's curse made her indestructible like me and the gods, but they can still hurt her. A lot.

"Let Cora help you, Arachne. Please."

"*They killed my family!*" she cries. Her scream rings in my ears. Zeroing in, my head hurts from the shock of her shriek. "All my little darlings! They're all gone! They're dead, Medusa! Dead! I had so many nests and they killed them all when they flooded the caves!"

What the fuck is she talking about?

Her darlings are her spiders, Gorgi.

I rub my ears. My ears are ringing and they hurt. I think she was loud enough for a human to hear her scream from up here. But then I hear the crickets again. And her quiet sobbing again.

"Oh, Arachne."

"Don't you understand? You loved your statues once in Sarpedon. I love my family. I talk to them. I care for them. Now they're all lost at the bottom of the sea. You told me to trust Cora. Well, Cora drowned her family and now mine! All the gods are bad. I told you already. I don't hold allegiance to any of them. But you know what? I have the Scepter. And no man can—"

"Even Hades will imprison you if you use the Scepter, Arachne."

"I don't care."

"Oh, God, babe, let this go," I plead. "Please. You have to. I know it hurts, but you have to."

"You don't know. Imagine all your statues being crushed at once before your eyes."

"Would your Christian God seek revenge?"

She leans back against the rail and actually snickers. Yeah, she actually laughs. "Clever. Clever and smart, Medusa. You are too smart. But not even that can convince me this time. Not after what they did."

"You chose this place to be alone and worship Jesus. You held a vow of silence for him. I respected that but came here to protect you. The Christian God you worship does not carry out vendettas. Christians don't take revenge. Your God turns the other cheek."

"All my nests are destroyed, Medusa!"

"When I had a chance to take revenge for us, Arachne, I didn't. If I had, I think it would have only made things worse."

"Do you know how many were killed when the walls fell? Thousands. Thousands of my little darlings. I'm sorry, but you don't understand. You can't. Every one of my darlings is...was like a person to me. And they're all gone."

"Please, Arachne, let me meet with you. Let's talk this over in person. You can have revenge, but let's do it the right way. A way that won't endanger you. Don't be hasty and anger both sides now."

"No."

"You will have to pick a side, Arachne," says another voice. My snakes turn before my head does. The voice is coming from above me, a half mile away. "Like me or not, we're on the same side. Come with me—"

"Some help you've been, Persephone!" Arachne looks toward the lighthouse. "Some help! My home is in ruins. My family is dead!"

"You know that wasn't by my hands."

"It was by your family!"

"Cora?" I say, sniffing up the hill and trying to zero in on her. "Cora, you're only going to drive her away."

"There isn't any more time, Gorgi," Cora says. "You think I'm the only one snooping in on this conversation? And it doesn't sound like your friend is unsure of her intentions."

"I'm not!" Arachne snaps. "*Flectere si nequeo superos, acheronta movebo!*"

She climbs over the rail beside the walkway.

"Arachne!" I cry.

I'm too late. She leaps into the water. She's gone under the docked boats.

"Cora!" I say, cocking my head back to the top of the mountain. "Why'd you do that! You made her run!"

"There's a team of Imada closing in on her by the harbor, Gorgi," Cora says with a sigh. "And, likely, Diana's nearby. I probably just saved her from being captured, like you did last night."

"Cora..." But I stop. If what she says is true, she did save her.

"I'm so sorry about what happened in the restaurant, babe," Cora says. "Don't worry, we covered it up. Any photos taken were destroyed."

"I don't care about me. I did it to get the attention off Arachne."

"I know you did. But you shouldn't have. Just like I told you that you shouldn't have come here."

"I have to help her. And, honestly, Cora, I think I was doing a better job talking to Arachne than you."

"I'm counting on that now. Since you're here, I need you to break through to her. We're not here to hurt her. We're here to help her. But, God, Gorge, that ends if she uses that weapon. If she uses the—"

"Just keep your distance. I'll do what I can."

It grows silent. I think Cora's left. But I finally locate her. I see a green schemata of her standing by the lighthouse looking out at the sea.

"I'm also watching your boyfriend," Cora adds. "Why the hell did you bring him here?"

"He snuck on the plane."

"We certainly know how to pick them, don't we?" Cora says with a laugh. "Good morning, Gorgi. Go get rest."

"Cora, if you or Hades do capture Arachne, you mustn't hurt her. Remember Sarpedon? They killed her spiders. They're just like what my statues were for me."

"She's right about me, Medusa. My family of monsters didn't only curse you, they cursed her. We are all bad and she has every right to hate me. But I owe Arachne, just like I owed you. I'm here for her, even if she can't stand me."

"Good morning, Cora."

"Good morning. I'm so sorry again about the restaurant. You were right, of course. My family is a bunch of idiots."

"But not you, Persephone. I love you."

"Take care of yourself. I love you too, babe."

I nod. Then I "sense" her leaving the lighthouse.

I glance back down at the bay. I search the dark water for Arachne, not with my eyes, but with my nose and hair. But Arachne's gone deep. She knows I'm not the only one who can detect her in the water. And she can stay underwater for hours.

The bay is so pretty with its lights like this at night. And now there's a dim glow of red off the horizon. If I weren't worried about my friend, I could stay.

Let's stay and watch the sunrise.

No, I'm so worried about her... I could find her. I could at least try?

Oh no. Oh no, you better not! Not in the water again!

But the first place she'll return to is that underwater statue. She'll swim right back under her God. And she'll swim fast. I can run the trail and get there faster.

You don't have a mask or snorkel!

So?

I don't want to feel that pain again!

This is for our friend. But boy, I really don't want to do it either.

Well? Ready? One step at a time. It's only like a five-mile run and a quarter-mile swim.

The sun's coming up, stupid.

I'm running.

I know the path. I walked it the first day after returning from my nighttime swim. I'm running faster than a wolf along the trail.

"Gorgi, forget it and turn around," says Cora's voice. "She's not going to be there." She's talking through the trees. "Agents are swimming around that statue right now. All you'll do is put yourself in danger."

I grind to a halt.

"Try to enjoy your holiday, babe," Cora says. "She'll turn up."

"But how can I help her? I'm so worried, Cora, you don't even know."

"Help her by enjoying your trip. Enjoy the town until she shows herself again. I have a feeling, from what she was saying, that it won't be long till we see her again."

6

AN ELOQUENCE IN TERROR

I'M WALKING THE WINDING PATH UP THE HILL ONCE MORE, this time holding hands with my man. I guide him through an alleyway beside another cute pink building, along a cobblestone street, and up a narrow private walkway that I found when I wandered around the other night. I know exactly where I'm going. To my right, behind some trees, is a steep drop off the hillside. There's a red line falling off the horizon into the sea. The sun is just creeping down under the water. We left our hotel room the minute it started getting dark.

I slept and I slept well during the day. God, the past couple days have been restless. But there's always time to sleep after vacation, I suppose. Now I'm trying to do what Cora suggested—enjoy my vacay. Lots of luck. My lover here is in even more trouble now.

Should I tell him about Arachne?

Just tell him.

But I'm worried he'll get into trouble if they catch him and question him.

Hey, wait. What am I saying! What do I mean "if they question him"?

Don't think about stuff like that!

Well, maybe I'm not telling him because I'm thinking he'll get mad.

He's the one who snuck along on the trip, Gorgi!

Fine. Just be quiet, Medusa.

My lover squeezes my hand to remind me he's walking beside me. Then I catch a glimpse of his incredible smile. God, I love him. I love just being with him, you know. Yes, I'm glad he came. I really am.

I turn another corner and Mr. Handsome follows. Then...voilà. We're here.

Shopping!

My panacea for all worry is this small nook of swanky shops along the main street. The shop I've been dying to go to looks quite ordinary. The clothes aren't. They've got all these summery clothes that are just to die for. The metal racks aren't very attractive, but the dresses and bathing suits are. The shop is almost empty. That's because it's closing time and it's a pretty quiet time of the year. One of the bummers here is that all the shops close early, which really sucks for a lamia-like night creature like myself.

Here's a large mirror near the cashier—a mirror I'm now using to do something I rarely do in public. Looking at myself. "So? What do you think?" I brush my long hair back with my hand. No bun tonight. Yeah, I'm on the wild side. "Well?"

I've got on this super gorge white cotton romper, cork sandals, and large shades. My boyfriend glances up from his cellphone.

"You'd look good in anything, Gorgiana."

So true. But I frown because I really want to know his thoughts.

"It looks really good on you," he adds with a smile.

"Thanks."

I look back in the mirror. No, no, it's...too good. This is why I wear granny pants in the library and keep my wigglies tied in a bun.

I'm back in the dressing room. My date's been a good sport. He's back to staring at his phone. I get it. We talked about dressing him up, but he complained so much that we shifted to me—which suits me fine.

Now I'm slipping on some white flip-flops. I look in the small mirror in the dressing closet. It'd be perfect if I didn't have my golden eyes. Now for the gray jump-suit. They've got a perfect matching wide-brimmed sun hat on a shelf by the front door that I think would look great with it. I can't wear hats, of course. My snakes would never be okay with that. As I fit into the jumpsuit, it's tight and pretty. It looks really good. No... I'd rather just try on this short-sleeved blouse with sky-blue shorts. That's cuter.

I'm back outside in front of the large mirror admiring the shorts. The nice old lady who owns the store nods as I stare at my bum. She also keeps looking at the door. I told you it is almost closing time.

"How about this one?" I ask.

"Sure, great, Gorge."

"Yeah." I check out my fanny again. "The other one looks better, honestly. And you're not even looking."

He looks up and flashes that smile that won my heart months ago. "Sorry. It looks good, Gorgi."

"'Kay."

But, no. No, I return to my dressing room, and put

the summery white romper on again. I'm thinking of buying this one instead.

As I'm sliding the romper up over my legs, there's a knock on my fitting room door. I figure it's the owner telling me to hurry.

"Gorgi," says my boyfriend. He sounds frantic. "Gorgi. Hurry. Something's up."

I hear murmuring outside. It's like the whole quiet town has become crazy.

"What's wrong?"

"Come out, quick."

Police sirens are blaring.

I throw down the romper and pull on my drab granny pants and sweater. Then I run outside.

There's so much shouting. The owner's at the front door watching. On the street, a bunch of people are rushing out from nearby stores and staring at the bay about a hundred yards below. I don't see anything weird. What's the fuss?

Police sirens blare again.

An elderly lady and an old man are pointing out the bay to some onlookers. Bright yellow floodlights from a helicopter hovering above reflect abnormally bright light along the water.

"What the hell's happening?" asks my boyfriend. "What happened to the water?"

What's wrong with the water?

I rush down the hill to get a better view and hear him following me. It's not one helicopter, but three, hovering over the water with searchlights. And the yellow lights keep focusing on a small black dot. But it's not a black dot. Focusing my cursed eyes, I recognize my friend Arachne.

She's standing on the water. She's standing because the water's gone. It's frozen solid into ice. She's wearing all black, a long white wig, and black gloves up to her elbows. She's bent over holding a reflective golden staff. The staff isn't just any staff—it's the scepter everybody's looking for.

A group of policemen on the beach are waving at her to get off the ice. She's not even looking at them. Her head remains bowed as she holds the staff.

A guy rushing to the harbor bumps into me from behind. Many people are running down to get a better look. The ships are locked in the harbor with icicles along their bow.

Red and blue lights reflect on the ice as more police on motorcycles approach the shore. Their sirens blare again. A few more officers join the others on the beach, gesturing for Arachne to get off the ice, but none of them has the courage to venture onto the ice-covered bay. They're rightfully fearful of the ice collapsing under her. But what they don't get is that the ice didn't appear from some weird freak storm in a cloudless sky. No. Of course not. It was formed by my spider friend— who's obviously lost her fucking mind—wielding a scepter.

She did it, Gorgi. They're going to bind her. Bury her forever.

Arachne raises her head and gazes right at me. Even from this far, like a mile out, she looks right at me amidst all the onlookers. A human would freeze. Not her. Her curse gives her just enough strength to stare right into my eyes. Then she smiles.

No. Don't.

I quickly shake my head.

Don't do it. Whatever the fuck you're planning, just don't do it.

I'm rushing, now running, dodging bodies, on my way to the bay. I've lost my boyfriend behind the crowds, but I can't care. By the time I stop near the ice, I expect Arachne to have done more damage. She hasn't. She's still crouched holding her gold staff, the Scepter, standing perfectly still.

My hair smells Persephone. Cora's standing close by the beach in that same red dress she wore the other night at the restaurant, folding her arms and staring at the harbor. Next to her, in a black suit, is that huge man: that creep Hades. The two gods don't look at me. They're staring at my crazy friend.

I run and stand beside them.

Then I sense another god. The only reason I can make her out is her disgusting smell. Diana. Diana's standing at the other end of the harbor, glaring at Arachne, about a hundred yards to my left.

Arachne stands up straight and raises her arms, as if preparing to dance.

No, don't do it!

But what's she doing? She's perfectly still, frozen in a dance pose, wielding the long gold scepter.

"What are you doing?" I ask aloud, making sure to talk right at her. I'm sure she can hear me, even from this distance, but she doesn't respond. She spreads her arms out wide. With her arms, six more black stubs unfold from behind. She's in her spider form, towering above the ice. Diana gasps and puts a hand over her mouth. She's one of the only ones. The other onlookers are too dumbfounded. Then Diana looks accusingly at me, as if I have something to do with this.

"What's she doing?" I cry to Cora. Cora shakes her head, still with folded arms, staring at her.

Arachne dips her body down and uses the sharp blades of her spider arms to push off the ice. Although she is hideous, her movement is graceful. Her body moves more smoothly than any Olympic figure skater. She rides across the bay with the tips of her black spider legs, quickly surpassing the police, passing a locked ship. Then she jumps in the air, performs an axel spin, and spreads her arms, drifting along the ice. A couple officers yell, but it doesn't stop Arachne from skating. Then Arachne kicks back and forth with her shoes until she has enough momentum to dig her spider legs into the ice. She jumps again, this time performing a double axel. The crowd cheers. Yeah, they actually cheer. Do they think this is some sort of fucking show? Can you believe it? Nearly everyone has their cellphones out taking pictures or videos. Some are just following the black figure with open mouths. Guys, this is Portofino, Italy, not vaudeville. Or Vegas.

"Release the nets," says Hades, talking into a hand-held walkie-talkie.

"What?" I ask.

He glances irritatingly at me.

"What's she doing?" I ask.

"What does it look like she's doing, Medusa?" Hades quips.

"Figure skating."

"You have to admit, she's good," says Cora with a nod and a chuckle. "Your friend always had style."

"Release the net," Hades says into his walkie-talkie again. "Apprehend her."

"What are you going to do to her?" I ask.

"She broke the law," Hades says. When he looks down at me, his eyes shine red. I spontaneously step back. "She's exposing you. Us."

"But her house was destroyed."

"Gorgi, we have to stop her," says Cora.

"What if she uses the Scepter against the helicopters?" asks Hades. "Or one of the tourists? We have to get it from her."

"But Imada destroyed her home!" I argue. "Your enemy killed her family. She's not thinking straight. You can stop her, but you guys have to understand her whole family was killed by Imada."

"I don't fucking care at the moment, Medusa," Hades says, finally turning to me. "She iced the Riviera."

"Let me just talk to her."

"You had your chance," Hades says, shaking his head. "Now the damage is done." Then he reaches back to his walkie-talkie. "Release the nets and immobilize her. Now!"

Nets are dropped from the chopper. They're white with thick rope. But they miss her. The black dot skates around them.

Then there's gunfire.

Are they shooting at her!

"Arachne!" I cry.

I catch Diana in my periphery across the harbor. She is looking right at me again. She looks frantic, speaking on her cellphone. She hates Arachne, like she hated the spiders on the table. She wants to crush her. But so do Cora and Hades. They all don't know her like I do.

I watch Arachne's face in the far distance with my

A+ predator eyes. She's not in distress. She's actually smiling, skating along the bay amidst gunfire as if it's all a game. I get it—she's showing everyone she's a spider. But, as I look at all the spectators, I wonder if her secret really is out. I wonder if she's revealing anything at all. I mean, I think people really believe this is some sort of bizarre show.

Arachne cuts the scepter deep into the ice, using it to launch herself into the air, then twirls and jumps with unbelievable finesse. Too unbelievable. There's no way a human could skate like that.

There's more applause. I mean, she deserves the accolades. She's amazing.

"Capture her," Hades snaps into his walkie-talkie again. "Stop this any way you can."

"No," I say, whirling around. "Don't hurt her."

Hades points to a guy with a thick vest, running with a large camera, at the other end of the bay. And another two guys carrying briefcases beside him. They stop by the shore's edge.

"That time Cora came down to save you in Sunland —do you remember, Medusa?" he asks. "I didn't come to help you. I was stopping Imada from revealing you. That was Athena's intention, you remember? To show you to the public and destroy your dull life. It wasn't about you, it was about us. Athena's intention of revealing you threatened all of us. Now your friend on the ice is doing the same."

I look back. But I laugh. I can't help it. I mean, she's really putting on a show now. It's ridiculous. It's ostentatious, and she's even shyer than I am.

But Hades is right. She said she planned to do something. This is the only revenge my friend could ever inflict on his invincible race. She can't hurt them, but she can reveal who they are.

Arachne stops. Then she stares right at me.

"What's she doing now?" asks Cora.

She dips down to the ice for a moment, then throws her body unnaturally high in the air once more, twisting, with all her legs this time, into an impossible axel. She starts spinning. After three spins, her dance becomes absolutely impossible. No human being could ever achieve this. I catch Hades's profile. His eyes scorch red.

"*Take her out now!*" Hades cries into his walkie-talkie.

She spins, over and over and over, and—

Another net is cast from a helicopter, this time landing right on top of her.

"Cora, are you going to hurt her?" I ask.

Cora cocks her head at me. "Gorgi, we need to stop her and get the scepter."

"But if you get it, will you just let her go?"

Cora shakes her head. She doesn't say anything. She doesn't need to. Of course, ignoring the question is enough.

I look back and Arachne struggles in the net. Without close focus, she's a black dot covered by a white net over white ice under floodlights. But with my snake eyes, I see her managing to break through some of the rope by cutting it with the sharp edge of the scepter, struggling to make her way out.

Maybe Arachne is right. Maybe my friends are no better than Imada?

"Medusa," Arachne finally whispers, right in my

direction. "You said you came to help me. Don't let them imprison me. Please. Please help me."

I look at Cora and she frowns sweetly at me. She heard her too. Well, Cora's pity isn't enough.

I jump over the wall of ice and slide along the ground.

"Gorgi, stop!" yells Cora. "Come back!"

"Get back!" cries Hades. "This is exactly what she wants!"

My tennis shoes slide like crazy along the ice. I fall. I use my fingernails, now sharp as knives, to claw through the ice and get up.

If your fingernails are getting long, that means—

Yeah, I'm turning full-on Medusa in front of the whole crowd. I know. But there's no way I can control my transformation now with all this excitement. Everybody's eyes are on me. Because I'm so terrified of this ice breaking and falling into the water. I don't want to drown again. It was so terrible. And now it's under freezing ice. I could fall through and drown at any moment. Not only that, I'm so worked up for my friend. But I have to help her. I just have to.

"*Enough nets, break the ice!*" thunders Hades behind me.

I slide toward Arachne. I fall. But I get up. And I keep falling again, and getting up again, over and over along the slippery ice. But every time I get up, I run like twenty miles an hour. I'm fast, very fast.

I've nearly reached her. I see Arachne's black body with normal focus now entangled under the white net. She smiles at me. She doesn't look distressed at all. The stupid crowd along the harbor roars with cheers of jubilation again—this time, I think, at me approaching her.

But then I hear explosions, like torpedoes from a ship. Geysers erupt in the ice around me. But they miss me and my friend. Why are they firing explosives?

I slip and pick myself up—for, like, the hundredth time—from the slippery ice. But then cracks surround the ice around me and Arachne. That means...

I'm in freezing water.

Fuck, it's cold! Not again!

I kick up water, gasping for air, through a hole in the ice. I squint my eyes from the yellow floodlight above. I search everywhere for my friend, struggling to stay near the surface. A couple more huge geysers erupt, one nearly overturning a boat. I catch a glimpse of rope underwater. I begin to swim to it.

Cold! So cold!

My body shakes in the freezing water. Not only did the ice freeze the surface, it made it cold underneath. But that means it must be warm further below.

I take a deep gasp of air, gulping in salt water, fighting my way forward, moving further down into a warmer darkness along the sea floor and using my eyes to light the way, like I did that first night.

Then everything turns from emerald to fiery red. There's an explosion as my body is hurled down into the water. My ears burst and ring. And fire lights the water above and flashes out in smoke and waves. I see what I think are helicopter blades crash into the water. Then comes the fuselage. There's another explosion and a fireball rushes toward me. Some of the fire burns my skin, causing searing pain.

A black figure, now blurry underwater, races to the

wreckage. The underwater arachnid tears open metal, pulling out a lifeless body. The spider surfaces, then submerges again. Arachne works at inhuman speed around the wreckage. She's moving men while I'm being pushed by a current to the sandy bottom.

Everything turns black...

There's another flash. I open my eyes but I can't see a thing. I'm blind. I think I was hit. I feel a sharp burn everywhere. My whole body feels as if it's encased in fire.

I can't breathe. I'm burning. I think parts of my body have been removed because, even with my beastly strength, I can't move a limb. It's dark. I can't breathe. I...

Shit, it's happening again!

7

SANTA

"Hɪ, Mᴇᴅᴜsᴀ."

My eyelids flutter open. I squint from a bright yellow light. It must be rays from the sun shining on my face. A figure stands over me, its dark shadow stretching across the white sand. Its back is turned. It's looking out over the waves. I have the taste of brine in my throat. It burns. My chest aches. My arms and legs throb. I feel sick.

I scream.

Then I vomit all over the sand, gasping for air.

The shadow doesn't turn. But she says, morose as hell, nodding a bald head, "You were right." I recognize her black skirt and leather top. It's Arachne, of course. "You were right."

I have no idea what the fuck she's talking about and, honestly, I don't give a shit at the moment. I feel horrible. I barf more. It feels like my stomach wants to turn inside out. I throw up more sand.

"Where are we?" I ask after a few more dry heaves. "Where have you taken me?"

"Santa," she says, turning with a rueful grin. Then she turns back to look out at the shore. "Bellissima Isola," she says quietly. "Santa."

It's an empty beach. There's just a bunch of sand and waves and a tall forested cliff behind me. But that's pretty. Very pretty. How is the sun out? Was I out for that long?

I put my head in my hands. That's when I notice my throbbing headache. I slowly rise to my feet. I'm wearing a wet black poncho—must be Arachne's. She must have dressed me after my body reconstituted. I was blown to bits, you know. At least, I think I was.

I approach Crazy, who's still enjoying the infinite ocean horizon.

"It's very pretty," I say.

"*Si, bellisimo,*" she says, cocking her head. I catch her bug eyes, but she's smiling at me.

"That was some fancy footwork back there."

"I practiced dance here and in secret places, over the centuries, where no one could see me. I love dance. The ice was trickier. Do you have beaches like this at home?"

"No."

So...we're engaging in small talk now?

"Life is shit." Arachne folds her arms with a nod and looks back at the lovely view.

"Why'd you do it, Arachne? What were you trying to achieve?"

"I wished to freeze Portofino and let the spider dance." She chuckles bitterly. Tears streak down her cheeks. "It was the only thing I could think of that would hurt their family for what they did to mine. But then the helicopter fell. A few men drowned under the ropes. Others were burned. I saved everyone I could. Those hurt or killed shall be added to the wrongs in my cursed life. I thought if I wielded the scepter, I'd be able to control it. That is why I took it. To protect it from evil. And look what I've done." She turns and looks at me so sadly I want to cry with her. "Oh, I'm sorry, Medusa, I'm so sorry. Forgive me. I was wrong. My spider appearance is *redicolo*—" She shakes her head. "I look so unreal that people thought it was a show. But you, when you appeared watching me... I thought, if I exposed *you*. I was so angry, I wanted to use you to show their presence in our world. I figured you'd come to rescue me. And you did. And then I could show Imada and your friends for what they are."

"Arachne, if you expose me, my life is ruined!"

"I know. I know. It was wrong."

She turns and weeps in her hands, facing the sea again.

Fuck! She can be so enraging.

Tear her apart! Punish her. How dare she?

I can't fight her. God, look at her, she's killing herself over it. I mean... I'm too weak anyway. She has her head in her hands, shaking. Well, I kinda feel like she deserves it this time.

But I say, "Everybody uses me. Don't feel so bad about it."

"That's because you are so nice," she says, with a nod, between sobs.

"How'd you find this beautiful place?" Small talk doesn't seem so bad to me anymore.

"I swim here often. It is Santa Margherita Ligure. After all the attention, I wanted to be alone. I wanted to be with you so I could apologize. You must hate me. You probably will never speak to me again."

"Oh, stop," I say, putting an arm around her then embracing her.

"Go home to your land in the sun," she says, squeezing me tight. "I shall return to my idol in San Fruttuoso and build another home under God."

"But, Arachne, I told you that you need to come back with me. You used the scepter. Now Imada *and* my friends will be after you. But if you return with me, I can find a way. I know Cora will protect you. She said she owed you. Even if she doesn't do it for you, she'll do it for me."

"No." She shakes her head. "No one cares about me, Medusa. If the scepter is out of my hands, they'll leave me and I will be happy alone." She reaches up and touches my hair. She gazes at it. I'm sure she can feel my wigglies stirring. My serpents adore the sun. "Go home. I'm so happy that you've found a small bit of happiness in your world."

"I'm so worried about you."

"I have God. When I said you were right, I didn't only mean about danger. My God does not believe in revenge. That is so. I shall surrender the scepter. I was never meant to be a guardian of such power. I know of only one person worthy of such power."

And she pulls out a tarantula from her wrist with a smile. It goes on her palm, and she presents it before me. I don't know where it came from. It's as if she performed a parlor trick to make it appear. To be polite, I pet the hairy beast. Ooh, but I'm sure my face has a really big scowl. *'Cause it's so gross!*

She laughs at my expression. "You are the best of

people, Medusa. You who they call a monster. Your name in the ancient tongue means 'guardian.' I can't carry this burden any longer. Of all people, I trust only you. If you ever leave your home in the States again, I welcome you back to Italia."

I hug her again.

"Bye, babe," I say.

But then I look around the shore and sigh. "But how the fuck do I get back home, Arachne?"

She laughs again. "Stay with me for a few hours along the beach, won't you? Please. Let us enjoy the sun together like the old days. I will get you back after."

"Sure, Arachne. Sure."

8

CUSTOMS

I'M WAITING IN LINE AT CUSTOMS AT THE INTERNATIONAL airport in Genoa to get on our flight back to the United States. I'm so tired. I was up all day with Arachne at that beach. Well, why not? I came here to see her, after all. But then it took me forever by boat to return to the hotel. Then I had to board a train to the airport. Now it's night, my usual awake time, and we're spending forever standing in this line.

My boyfriend yawns.

"Oh, *you're* tired?" I say. "Please."

"It was a fun time, Gorgi," he says, finishing another yawn. "Thanks for not turning me away."

"How could I? You bought your ticket behind my back."

"Yeah, but you didn't tell me to leave. And it was so much fun, wasn't it?" He kisses my cheek.

No, not really. But I say, "yes." And I snuggle in his arms.

"I wish you could have enjoyed it like I did."

Of course, he knows everything now. After the

whole jump onto the ice under helicopters thing, it was hard to avoid talking about Arachne. And he's already met Cora and Hades. So he knows my trip was complete shit. Now I just want to get through all these lines and head back home, where it's safe.

Then, wouldn't you know it, he points to a TV screen mounted on a wall in the airport. It shows helicopters hovering over ice. There's a dark speck, my friend Arachne, skating with her spider legs in the center. They throw the white-roped nets. My body with granny pants and a sweater appears, jumping on the ice, for a split second, then the footage stops. It's not long enough for anybody to see my hair, thank God. Hades had his hands in that. The camera then pans to the ice, and everything collapses. Water is thrown in the air, and the docked boats are seen rocking like crazy from the resulting turbulence in the bay.

Portofino. I don't think my experience was quite like any other.

"Can I see your bag, signora?" asks an officer. We're at the front of the line. She gestures to a table and is all smiley.

Uh-oh.

I was dreading this. I'm not a very good smuggler, you know. I'm a very neat person, but I tried to make my bag a mess so no one digs too deep.

I slowly pull the bag off my shoulder and unzip it for her on the table. She rummages around my compact mirror, extra shirt, shoes, cellphone chargers, laptop, and gold staff...oh, yeah, there's a shiny gilded staff hidden at the bottom. It's shrunk now, another magical thing the thingy can do, so it fits in my bag snugly. But the officer opens her eyes wide.

"Is that the—" my boyfriend says with wide eyes over my shoulder.

Before he can speak another word, a stunningly lovely lady with long blond hair and bright blue eyes in a white customs officer uniform glides over and touches my hand. She returns the golden rod snugly to my bag and zips it up. Then she says to the other officer with a smile, "*Va bene, non fa niente.*"

The other officer nods.

"Cora?" asks my boyfriend in disbelief.

Cora winks at him. Then she says in a very fake Italian accent, "Enjoy your flight back to America."

THE END

Gorgiana and Cora continue their Greek mythological mayhem in the 21st century in "Furies":

- MY EVIL EYE
- NECTAR OF AMBROSIA , a novella
- CORA

PARTING WORDS

What did you think of *The Guardian*? By placing a book review, you can inform others of your thoughts and help spread the word about my book.

Want more? Periodically I like to send news regarding current or new projects. If you'd like to be privy, I encourage you to sign up to my email newsletter. Your information will remain private and you can cancel any time.

Sign up at www.alhawke.com or scan the following QR code:

EXCERPT FROM MY EVIL EYE

THE FOLLOWING EXCERPT IS FROM "CHAPTER 1 - FUGU TIME" IN MY EVIL EYE, FROM THE FURIES SERIES BY A.L. HAWKE

They always look at me funny. Whenever I roll my cart down the aisles shelving books, readjusting my glasses over my nose, or even just typing on the computer, boys look at me weird. Somehow they know I don't quite fit in. I know. I don't. But you know, to monsters, it's the normal people that are the weirdos.

There's one now. Look at him. He's just leaning against a wall with his sweaty armpit over the nose of a poor blonde in a cute sky-blue university sweater who's trying to study. She doesn't look like the type that normally studies—neither does the jock—but this is dead week, when students actually have to. She's trying to humor him by looking up and smiling, but I know she really wants him to leave her alone.

Don't look at him. Forget about him.

I shake my head and shelve a heavy textbook.

I'm in the main hall of Sunland University's library. It's a grand retro-nineteenth-century hall with loads of walnut columns and bookshelves and a vaulted dome ceiling. On one side is a waterfall. Yeah, an actual waterfall. And they have plants surrounding it, which I love because with the lighting and foliage, it makes me feel I'm outdoors and it's daytime. I like to read here late at night when I finish work early. On the other side of the hall is a bunch of offices behind windowed walls. Everything's lit by modern-looking chandeliers.

Shit, there's another creep bugging the girl. This ape won't stop fucking slapping her shoulder. I always perk up when guys act like this. I was violated in Sarpedon eons ago, you know. Even a little playing around is *not okay*.

Hey, don't look at me. Don't do that!

What a bunch of assholes.

Calm down, Gorgi.

Well... Don't fucking look at me!

He turns. Then he leans over and whispers something to her. I move my wigglies back from my ear to snoop.

"Come on. You want the stuff or not?"

"Give it to me or just leave me alone, Carl."

The guy standing over her looks right at me.

Keep your eyes off me!

My gaze is deadly, you know. It's like Fugu. Do you know what Fugu is? Fugu in Japanese translates to "fortune." It's the puffer fish. The puffer fish is a delicacy that tastes wonderful but, if not prepared just right, the poison doesn't give you good fortune. I've tried Fugu. It's not *that* great, even when prepared right. I've had it prepared wrong too. (It tastes the same, by the way.) Anyway, my eyes are like Fugu. They lure you in, entice you, but if you enjoy too much...bye, bye. Hey, what a coincidence—I'm shelving a book on Japanese cuisine.

"Excuse me?" Someone is tapping on my shoulder.

I whirl around. Being an A+ apex predator, it's rare that someone sneaks up on me, but I was distracted by the jerks.

"Can you help me with my book search?" he asks.

It's this tall guy with wavy golden hair thrown to the side. His face is a little sunburnt. He's wearing a button-down and baggy pants. He's got broad shoulders and strong arms. He's grinning. And he's cut and he's, *uh, hmm,* hot.

Oops. He opens his eyes wide. Did he see my cursed eyes? No, he's looking over at those two assholes laughing at the girl.

"I—" He coughs. "I figured you work here?"

"I do," I say, looking down at the floor.

"Can you help me? I'm in this Western Civ class, and the professor's asking for us to check out a book. I think she thinks it's like an inside joke. I mean, who checks out books at a library anymore when there's the web? No one. It's kinda stupid."

"There's lots of stuff in books you can't find online."

"Oh," he says, looking flustered. "Of course, *a librarian* would say that." He stops talking. I think it's because I'm staring at the ground.

Yep, he leans down to look into my eyes. I turn away.

"Are you okay?" he asks.

I nod. But I don't look at him. I want to. I really do. I already caught a glimpse of his strong jawline, five o'clock shadow, perfect teeth, and kind smile.

"I was just saying we could google it," he continues, rubbing his neck. "But the professor wants us to use the library. I've seen you working here before. You're one of the librarians. Right?"

"Yes."

He smiles again. He has such a cute smile. It's telling me he's not really here to search for books, you know.

Shit, did he catch a glimpse of my Fugu? Is that it? I wear these thick spectacles with special lenses to hide my golden gems, but they're not perfect. If a guy gazes straight into my eyes, it's Fugu time. Particularly if my gold gems turn green. Sometimes somebody catches a glimpse from the side. Many years ago, I went to an optician to fit me with trick glasses that would be clear for me but blurry straight on for wandering eyes. I've tried lots of ways to hide my cursed eyes. Opaque shades work too, but Charlie, he's my boss, wouldn't take kindly to his librarians wearing sunglasses at work.

"Can you help me?" Oh yeah, the blond guy's still talking to me.

He follows me down three steps into another part of the library I love, with the gorgeous fountain I was talking about. The fountain has lovely trickling water. It's made of white stone and, I mean, it's not the Trevi Fountain, more of a tacky bozzetto, but I absolutely adore it. It was here decades ago when I applied for the job. I think it's what sold me. And tables circle the fountain, with computers where you can search for stuff. Students also sit on the three steps, but they're nearly always empty when I work here at night.

I sit down in front of a large antique monitor.

"What would you like to search for?" My eyes are focused on the screen.

His sunburnt hand is beside mine. Mine, peeping out from my ugly thick furry brown sweater, hovering over the keyboard, is tanned, always the same olive color, sun exposure or not. I don't burn—or, when I do, it just goes back to the same color. He has strong hands. Cute, nicely groomed strong man hands.

"Genghis Khan," he says, leaning over my shoulder.

"Genghis Khan," I say, typing fast. "This is similar to a google search. It's easy. You just type your word. You get the location here and the ISBN. Get it?"

"What's an ISBN?"

"It's an identifier. All books have them."

I feel tingles sitting near him. And I hear his heart jump a little. And his scent, his essence is... *like ...*

"Excuse me for not knowing what an ISBN is," he quips.

"Well..." I brush my bangs from my eyes with a smile. "Once you find the location, you can look for it by subject. We use the Library of Congress classification system here, not the Dewey Decimal. See, this shows a map of our library and where each category of books is shelved. And here's a call number for a book. Easy, right?"

"Easy for you."

He is staring at my profile. I turn a little so he doesn't see my eyes.

"You really like this stuff, don't you?" he asks.

"I love books."

"*Come on!*" snaps one of the meatheads in a forced whisper. I had totally forgotten about them. "*Hand it over or forget the whole thing.*"

"*Just leave her alone, Carl.*"

"*Let me go. Here's the money.*"

Let me go?!

I look up. I can't see anything past the fountain, but I can smell them. With my nose, I sense a hand yanking his prey's arm. My wigglies fight to break out from their cage in my hair. I press down on my bun. Then I glance back at the boy beside me. He's none the wiser, but he's squinting at me.

"Genghis Khan?" he asks, raising his brow.

"Oh." I start typing fast again. "Here's a directory of over twenty books on the subject. Just go to the third floor and find this section." I tap the screen. "I'll print out a list of call numbers for your report."

I quickly get up, looking toward the commotion.

"Can you show me the location upstairs?"

"What?" I ask, turning back to him with a laugh. "It's easy."

"Easy for you."

"Let me go! Where are you taking me!"

That fucker is tugging her arm! Can you believe this? That fucking dick is pulling her! I sense the whole building like a green schemata in my mind. And the angrier I get the clearer the image becomes.

I've had enough. I rush up the steps from the fountain back up to the main hall.

"Oh...well, thanks," blurts the student.

"Let me go, Carl!"

Let me go?!

I hear the struggle through the walls. They've left the main hall. No one else has any idea this commotion is going on. The struggle isn't loud; it's more like forced whispers. But the girl's panic rings in my ears.

When I was in Sarpedon, I was tricked by the slick,

sugary tongue of Poseidon. And the horror began when the god grabbed my wrist. It's been thousands of years, but as the girl is dragged, I feel her pain as if he's dragging me by the arm.

I need to calm down. I can't change in front of these kids.

But he touched her. He's forcing her!

My hair is aching to escape its hair tie. My incisors are digging into my lower lip. I grasp my hands tightly, trying to distract myself, telling myself not to change— not to do that in front of all these students. But I want to hurt him.

I hear a body being thrown against a wall. It's a faint sound. My eyes are burning like green flashlights through my spectacles. Bright emerald. I shade my eyes as I break out into a run.

I hear a shirt tear. And she cries out as he twists her arm again.

Oh, you going to do that? Huh? Okay, you know what I'm going to do? I'm going to dislocate your wrist, pull your hand from its socket, and stuff it down your motherfucking throat!

I rush down a hallway that connects the library to a nearby lecture building. A girl by the library exit, who's standing by a table reading, stares up at me as I sprint past her. Her human ears probably don't hear the struggle.

Everything turns dark and empty as I enter the corridor into the lecture hall. I follow their scent into another hallway. Then one more turn. And then...

I throw open the door to a boy's bathroom. It's empty. But there's movement in one of the stalls. I rush over and pull at the stall door. It's locked. I easily break the metal door open.

The asshole has the girl bent over facing the toilet. He doesn't even stop groping her—he's locked in predatory mode. Her shirt is torn, revealing bare breasts, and he's dropped his pants. He looks over his shoulder. Actually, they both do.

What a sight I must be. I'm not covering my green eyes anymore. Their bodies are illuminated in green light.

"Go," I say to the girl. "Get out of here."

The girl nods, clutching her torn shirt over her chest. She runs past me to the exit in tears. I turn to the creep. He's such a pompous ass that he faces me, still bathed in green light, with his cock wagging.

I'm feeling pain in my wrist. Is it my ancient memory of Greece? Or is it my empathy for the girl?

She's gone. It's over. Just let him go.

Uh... Nuh-uh.

I smile lasciviously at the boy. I remove my ugly brown sweater. I take off my shirt and bra and lay them gently by the sink. I take my time getting naked in front of him. Let him relish my poison. He's frozen after seeing my eyes.

"Is this what you wanted?" I ask. I slowly back away. "A nude girl?"

He gazes at my body with wide eyes. He doesn't seem to care that I look like a demon from hell right now, with fangs, sharp fingernails, and green, glowing eyes. He wants a taste of my body. A taste of my delicious Fugu. And, boy, is he gonna get it.

His body, though frozen, trembles.

"Who are you?" he asks, struggling to move his mouth. "*The librarian?*"

"I'm the devil."

I walk up to his ear and lick it. Then I brush my palm along his bushy beard and brush my tits against his side. "You want to sin? Sin with me. I'm not innocent. I can show you a good time."

"Sure," he purrs.

I run my hand along his shirt. His hands are weak, so I help him lift it. Then my hand runs over the bulges of his huge pecs. I pull the pants, still bunched around his ankles, away from his feet. Now he's naked and dirty, just like the filthy motherfucker he is.

But I freeze for a moment. I clutch my head in my hand... What am I doing? The girl's gone. She's safe. I can just stop. Right?

NO! He was bending her over like a dog! You gonna let a man do that? After all that's happened to you?

I run my lips along his. Then I slowly wrap my fingers around his wrist. I twist. I could yank his hand right off with one more turn. Oh, it'd be so easy.

Cut it off and stuff it down his motherfucking throat!

No. I... I can't do that.

He winces and writhes as I twist. Then he shrieks. His body jerks to nurse his injured hand, but he can barely move.

"Why'd you do that?" he asks.

I giggle.

"What's your name?"

"Medusa."

My tongue comes out, forked like a snake's tongue, at the utterance of my ancient name. It licks his cheek and ear. But my long serpent tongue doesn't bother him the slightest bit. I reach back with my free hand, as I continue to stroke his cheek with the other, and finally free the bun from my head.

Oh, what a relief! As the bun unfolds, my black hair falls, freeing my friends, and the snakes thicken, slithering and slinking over my face. I take a deep breath as my beasties are let loose. Some of the black snakes run along his face. A couple even loop around his neck. I could choke and suffocate him. I've done it before. He's already too far gone to resist.

I should just snap his neck and be done with him.

No. Tease him. Make sure he's just conscious enough to feel the pain he brought her.

"You naughty, naughty boy," I whisper in his ear. I run my forked tongue along his ear. "How could you do that to an innocent girl?"

"Oh, she's not innocent," he says with a chuckle. My forked tongue enters his mouth and wraps around his tongue. I could constrict it and remove it.

Don't. Not yet. Play with him first.

I pull back from his lips, but it takes all my will to not pull out a chunk of his face.

"She was cheating on me," he says.

"Cheating on you? A virile young man? I don't believe it. So you were going to force a fuck?" At the word *fuck* his body shakes. "Because she deserved it?"

He chuckles nervously.

"Did she force the other boy to have sex too?"

"They met at a hazing," he says. His head is immobile. Only his mouth moves. "My friend met up with her after to study." I run my hand along his thick beard again. I hear his heart beating like crazy. "Next thing I knew I saw them screwing on my bed. So what I did was I planned this whole deal. I wanted to teach her a lesson and show her who her true boyfriend really is. My way. I figured the bathroom was private." He looks at my eyes, but I don't meet his gaze. There's enough green from my eyes in the room to entrance him. A little more and he wouldn't be able to move his mouth and finish his stupid excuse. "I guess... not so private."

"Touch my hair," I say. "Go on."

He lifts a shaky hand and runs his fingers along my hair. My vipers coil around them. Perhaps this would be enough? I can sever his fingers and leave him with a maimed hand? That would teach him a lesson, wouldn't it?

No. Kill him! Kill him!

"Well, you told me your story, my boy, why don't you let me tell you mine?" I cuddle his head on my breasts. "I'm going to give you quite a whopper."

"It was three thousand years ago. I worked in the temple of Athena. I was a priestess. Every day I toiled hard maintaining the goddess's great temple. I was a model priestess. Of course, I was a virgin. All those who worked the great temple of Athena were virgins. God forbid we were ever *fucked*..." His body shakes again. "Or defiled by horny boys."

I guide his hand along my side, and his fingers somehow manage to twitch along the crack of my ass. It makes me almost furious enough to finish him.

"I'm not done," I say, moving his hand from my butt. "Listen. One day, as I was out to gather water from the well, I was surprised by a voice. It was a stranger flattering me over my beauty. I had always known I was pretty. In fact, many think I am the most beautiful woman in the world. In fact, it was my beauty that drew so many other virgins to the temple. That was good for business, but bad for the goddess Athena's jealousy."

"Yes, you are hot," he mutters stupidly.

"Aha. The voice was Poseidon's. The god had seen me alone and came to me when I was vulnerable. The god grabbed my arm and tore off my sacred white robe and fucked me right there by the well. He fucked me like no man had ever fucked before. He was a mighty Olympian god, after all. He showed her who was boss, just like you were doing to that poor girl. Right?"

I laugh. There's really nothing funny about that. But it's too bad for him that he's too entranced to join me in my mirth. If he chuckled, that would be another reason for me to finish him off. Instead, the fucker finds the strength to lower his head and run his lips around my nipples.

Go ahead and suck. That's fugu too.

"Well, the very next morning, I ran. I ran from the temple because I had been defiled. My mere presence dirtied the sacred ground, and it was a grievous insult to the goddess Athena. I didn't get far. Athena came to me personally. She tripped me with Apollo's snakes."

I grab his cock. I pull a little, like I pulled his wrist. He winces. He leaves my tit and leans into my face, pressing his lips into mine. Apparently, he didn't notice my sharp fangs and slithering vipers.

"She turned me into one," I say with a shrug, between his kisses. "Ever since then, I've borne witness and left alone all sins. I turn my eyes from theft, adultery, even murder. But never, ever, ever do I avert my eyes from one sin. Do you happen to know what that sin is?"

He shakes his head.

"Rape," I say. "Rape is one thing I will never witness again. When Poseidon pinned me, and the stars sent me no mercy, and when, instead of judging a god and punishing Poseidon, the gods turned on an innocent young girl and ruined her, I realized there is no one in this whole fucking world that cares about me. I have been discarded. Trash. For me, I'm done. But for another, no. I vowed to never, ever, ever, let that happen to another lady in my presence. Do I make myself clear?"

He nods with a smile, looking at me—full of desire —thinking somehow, weirdly, that I'm going to have sex with him. If someone were to walk in now and witness my fangs, my moving hair, and my glowing red eyes beside him, they might think this is funny. You do, right? But it really isn't amusing, is it?

He deserves punishment. Punish him.

The snakes in my hair move in a fury, hissing wildly. My eyes glow a brighter green, illuminating his whole face. When I am ready for the kill, I lose all attractiveness. But the boy seems too deep in his trance to notice.

"Now, tell me, what were you doing to that poor girl?"

He laughs. Then he gazes into my eyes and a shadow seems to fall over him. That's what I was waiting for. Realization. With my seduction, I've unleashed the lamia of his destruction. I am revenge. He loses all mirth. Well, like I said, there was nothing funny here. There never was. I reach down and grab his penis and...it's all over.

Look into the eyes of Medusa. Gaze into me as I ravish you. Keep your eyes on mine as your skin tears from your neck, shredding muscle and sinew, leaving your chest bloody and back bare. Your flesh I rip. Your arms and legs I tear. I dismember you into the heap of shit you are.

Still awake? Good. Feel more... Pain!

I should just leave him. She's gone and...

Take his hand and shove it down his throat!

His screams are muffled. His cries seem to be coming from so far away, as if in a faraway tunnel. At this point, I'm far into a trance myself.

And...

I black out. But, in my periphery, I watch a body fall to the floor—in pieces.

In the back of my mind, I recall screaming. Is it a memory or is it happening now? I'm not sure.

As I awaken further, I take a deep breath. I feel dizzy.

I walk to the bathroom mirror. Red is splashed on my face. I wash my face. As the crimson washes away and the snakes recede, my face is absolutely beautiful again. The prettiest face in the world. I arrange my hair back in a bun.

The metallic stench of his blood has taken the place of piss and shit and fills the bathroom. I walk to the door and realize I crushed the doorknob after the girl ran. Then, as I awaken more, I realize a bunch of people are banging on the door.

My God, what have I done? In my periphery, I see crimson flesh smeared and heaped against the white tile. There's only a mound of meat on the floor, no recognizable body.

There's a window on the other end of the bathroom. It's just big enough for us to slither through.

Go, Medusa! Run!

MEDUSA'S ADVENTURE CONTINUES IN MY EVIL EYE, THE FIRST BOOK IN FURIES

ALSO BY A.L. HAWKE

PARANORMAL ROMANCE

- MY EVIL EYE
- THE GUARDIAN
- NECTAR OF AMBROSIA
- CORA

- ALONDRA
- HAWTHORNE UNIVERSITY WITCH SERIES I-III
- HAWTHORNE UNIVERSITY WITCH SERIES 4-6
- THE HAWTHORNE UNIVERSITY WITCH HOLIDAY COLLECTION

- SHADES
- HAUNTING JOY
- PHANTOM MASQUERADE

FANTASY: THE AZURE SERIES

- HARMONIA
- CORA: RISE OF THE FALLEN GODDESS
- AZURE BLUE
- CORAL RED
- PRINCESS SOJOURN

SCIENCE FICTION

- CANDY SAVANT SERIES

Books available at https://alhawke.com/books

ABOUT THE AUTHOR

A.L. Hawke is the author of the bestselling Hawthorne University Witch series. The author lives in Southern California torching the midnight candle over lovers against a backdrop of machines, nymphs, magic, spice and mayhem. A.L. Hawke writes fantasy and romance spanning four thousand years, from pre-civilization to contemporary and beyond.

Visit A.L. Hawke at www.alhawke.com

Email: contact@alhawke.com